W9-AKB-371

J.
R

11,959

Rice, Eve
   What Sadie sang. Story and pictures by Eve
Rice.   N.Y., Greenwillow books, [1976]
  unp.   col.illus.

   1.Infants-Fiction.   I.Title.

EAU CLAIRE DISTRICT LIBRARY

WHAT SADIE SANG

Story and pictures by Eve Rice

GREENWILLOW BOOKS • A Division of William Morrow & Company, Inc. • New York

EAU CLAIRE DISTRICT LIBRARY
77767

Copyright © 1976 by Eve Rice
All rights reserved. No part of this
book may be reproduced or utilized
in any form or by any means,
electronic or mechanical, including
photocopying, recording or by any
information storage and retrieval
system, without permission in
writing from the Publisher. Inquiries
should be addressed to Greenwillow
Books, 105 Madison Ave., New
York, N.Y. 10016. Printed in the
United States of America.

1   2   3   4   5   80   79   78   77   76

Library of Congress Cataloging
in Publication Data

Rice, Eve.   What Sadie sang.

Summary: Even though Sadie's
song is only one syllable, it means
many things to her and her mother
as they go for a walk.
[1.   Infants—Fiction]   I.
Title.   PZ7.R3622Wh   [E]
75-33244   ISBN 0-688-80038-6
ISBN 0-688-84038-8 lib. bdg.

For T.D.M.M.D.

Sadie could walk all by herself.

But today she did not want to walk.

So Mama put Sadie in her stroller.

"There," said Mama.

"Ooooh!" said Sadie.

Mama pushed.
The sticky stroller wheels
went click, click, click.
"Gheee!" said Sadie.

And "Gheee, gheee, gheee!"
"What is the matter?" asked Mrs. Finley.
"Is Sadie crying?"

But Sadie was not crying. She was singing.
And she sang "Gheee, gheee, gheee" again.

Sadie sang to the tree on the corner

and to the red, red fire hydrant,

to a new spring tulip in a tub,

and to a scratching shaggy dog,

who said "Woof" in return.

And the grocer said,
"Maybe it's a toothache."

But Mama did not worry.

She knew a song when she heard one.

Sadie sang as they went to the river—

for the chugging tugboat

and the circling seagull.

Now "Gheee, gheee, gheee" was a river song.

Mama turned the stroller around
and Sadie kept right on singing,
so then it was a going-home song.

It was a very good going-home song
because Sadie was still singing
when Mama unlocked the front door.

"There," said Mama. "Naptime."

"Ummmm," said Sadie.

And she sang "Gheee, gheee, gheee"
all the way up the stairs

and into bed.

"Gheee, gheee, gheee," sang Sadie.

But that was the end of the song…

because Sadie was asleep.